THE FURIOUS FLYCYCLE

JAN WAHL

Copyright © 1968 by Jan Wahl

Cover and interior art by Ted Enik

A Tor Book
Published by Tom Doherty Associates, Inc.
175 Fifth Avenue
New York, N.Y. 10010

Tor® is a registered trademark of Tom Doherty Associates, Inc.

ISBN: 0-812-52404-7

First Tor edition: April 1994

Printed in the United States of America

0 9 8 7 6 5 4 3 2 1

to my good brother

ROBERT

*T*he house in town that had the most shutters, a spooky turret, a cat named Tweet about to have babies, an ancient spreading apple tree with lots of red apples, and a barn in back with spires sticking up and fancy woodcarving, was the house on Bean Road in which lived Melvin Spitznagle.

Melvin was considered lucky: his father owned the Ice Cream Works on Radish Street, where they wholesaled and manufactured Spitznagle's Ice Cream. There was a freezer with a capacity of six tons a day; and the business included a fifteen horsepower engine. The annual output was between

twenty thousand and thirty thousand gallons. It was the most important ice cream works in the County. Melvin liked to walk past the big plant and read the sign, with letters in faded gold and blue, that said:

SPITZNAGLE'S ICE CREAM
"Better than it sounds"

Because his father was the ice cream maker, Melvin grew pretty popular at school. His father brought home, in five-gallon containers, the ice cream not sold to stores within a week. So Melvin's schoolmates trooped hungrily off to Bean Road after school, and they would sit on the white-painted benches and lawn chairs in the Spitznagle back yard politely but eagerly, wondering which flavor Emma Dudd, the maid, was going to bring out. It was vanilla most often.

But with jams and sauces and different syrups (which they brought with them) added, Melvin's schoolmates could vary the flavors as they chose. Emma Dudd was kept busy zipping back and forth from the kitchen, and usually her linen maid's cap fell over her eyes as she hurried.

Thus Melvin never lacked for company.

However, in his heart, he wished he were enjoyed for himself alone; with the result that suddenly one day he asked his father to give the unsold ice cream, in its five-gallon containers, to the county Orphan Asylum instead. Nobody much came to the back yard after that, except two fat little girls, the Sprenger sisters, Mavis and Edna—who wanted to play croquet.

Melvin said "Pooh Pooh!" to everybody and decided to spend his time becoming a scientific mechanical wizard.

He was handy at repairing bicycles. And people soon began showing up with broken chains and sprung sprockets for him to fix. Again, however, Melvin began to feel he was not being appreciated for what he was himself.

So he pleaded with his parents and got them to let him use the unused barn for his private workshop.

He outfitted the place with wonderful

tools—handdrills, wrenches, pronged and prongless hammers, pliers, vises, screwdrivers, files, saws, chisels, soldering irons, and other things.

On the door he put a sign:

BEWARE!! GROUCHY PERSON

Soon he became skilled at searching around in gutters and trash heaps where he located cast-off rubber, tinfoil, odd pieces, copper kettles (to be melted down), all of which he would put to use.

He connected a telegraph system from the barn to the kitchen, in case he was knee-deep in work, not able to join his family at dinner. Emma Dudd was very slow to learn—though she managed to understand the simplest of messages. Emma was not very good at sending messages back because she had a tendency to get terribly nervous.

TWO HOURS AGO ON THE NOSE WE EAT was one message Emma sent to the barn. COME NOW SEE YOUR MOTHER HAD KITTENS was another.

Of course it was Tweet who had the kittens. In the pantry.

There were five babies. One black. One white. One black and white spotted. One black with gray stripes. One gray with white,

white ruff. When the gray one grew big enough, Melvin took it for his mascot. He decided to call it Spunky.

In the evenings Mr. Spitznagle would sit in the large overstuffed armchair in the living room comfortably reading a book, smoking smelly cigars. Mrs. Spitznagle would sit at a wobbly-legged walnut desk, writing letters to all her relatives—there was nothing she liked better than receiving a batch of mail. Emma Dudd would be dreamily doing dishes in the kitchen.

Melvin, however, would be hard at work out in the barn at his workbench while Spunky played with a cotton ball near his feet. Even when a rainstorm beat down on the barn roof, wind howling at every corner, Melvin worked steadily on, learning something new every day.

When Emma Dudd was missing the eggbeater, she knew where it had gone. When Melvin's mother's sewing machine was missing some of its parts, she knew where they had disappeared to.

Yet always, when Melvin returned a thing (which he did, having learned its secret), it was better than new; he *was* a mechanical wizard. The eggbeater then became the fastest in town, the sewing machine stitched quicker and better than before.

One hot July day the freezer at his father's plant broke down. The ice cream came flooding out in a huge mound onto Radish Street.

The town fire department arrived, starting to work with shovels. Soon, all the dogs and cats in town heard about it and were there, licking up the rainbow-colored treat— the cherry, peach, lime, vanilla, strawberry, chocolate!

Melvin raced across town with his tool kit. He went straight to the source of the trouble—a loose rotary four-gauge Whirlogax, pulled out his #7 roman wrench, and, in a

jiffy, had everything under control. The fire department stood there amazed. Mr. Spitznagle did not have to send his employees home.

A few days later a truck pulled up on Bean Road.

The expressman wheeled up to the door a dazzling object—a new Silver Zephyr bicycle. Attached to it was a tag reading IN GRATITUDE. YOUR FATHER.

Melvin took a few days off from his workshop to pedal the Silver Zephyr up and down the streets. He even went outside of town, trying country roads. There the riding got bumpy. Melvin wished he were able to ride as fast as a tornado. He drove everywhere with a dreamy look in his eyes, narrowly missing flocks of chickens and yipping dogs; Melvin was lost in thought.

Then Fate stepped into his life. Fate was an old, old man in battered top hat and shaggy beard.

Professor Mickimecki, with beard, top hat, with a red-bulb nose, with his hose torn, wearing worn carpet slippers in place of shoes, the great inventor Professor Mickimecki (for-

11

merly of Prague, Stuttgart, Liverpool, and Bombay) had shot through town on the Rapid Pearl Express, which came through once a week without stopping on its way to points West.

As the train raced through, Professor Mickimecki had pulled the emergency cord. "STOP THE TRAIN!" he shouted, tossing his valises out the window to the surprise of fellow passengers.

Then he scrambled out himself, holding onto his top hat.

"This is the town in which I want to spend the rest of my life. *Unnoticed!*"

That very same afternoon the Professor rented, with one hundred dollars down in two-dollar bills, the old Ketcham house.

Soon he painted the house green, so that it looked like grass. The fleet of trucks that came bringing his many large crates and boxes had a hard time finding it.

It was an inspiration to Melvin just to know so great a man lived now in town.

He would wander by after dusk and station himself across the street, hiding under a willow tree growing there. Through the willow branches he would watch. The Professor

13

had had constructed, on top of the high gabled green roof, a gigantic windmill—obviously a part of his experiments.

The windmill would creak and spin on the roof. A wide skylight had been put in to the right of the windmill; sometimes, even before the sun went down, there was a red glow from beneath. Green and yellow sparks would fly up the chimney mysteriously.

It made Melvin quite happy and quite sad to see all this, since he was hiding under the willow tree, while the Professor was hiding inside his house, and it seemed unlikely that the two should ever meet.

One morning Melvin asked his mother, "Do you suppose you could make me a green-colored suit?" He believed in that way he could get closer to the Professor's house—for he could walk then around the yard and look inside the windows.

However, Mrs. Spitznagle did *not* want to make a green-colored suit. So Melvin had

to remain under the willow tree worshipping from afar.

The days passed slowly.

Melvin would read *The Evening Star*, the town weekly newspaper, carefully, hunting for mention of Professor Mickimecki. But the Professor seldom came out of his house, and certainly never gave interviews to *The Evening Star*.

Spunky grew into a faithful cat, following Melvin around like a dog. Spunky learned to jump out of the way when Melvin bustled around in the workshop. At night Spunky slept at the foot of Melvin's bed. Melvin learned how to crawl out of the gray cat's way in his sleep so that he sometimes woke up locked in the shape of the letter Z.

It was at Gearhart's Hardware Company that the paths of Melvin and Professor Mickimecki crossed. Melvin had bicycled uptown to purchase a few nuts and bolts. He was looking around admiring many objects in the store, when in bounced the bearded

Professor demanding, "Give me a reel of piano wire!"

"Yes sir!" said Anton Gearhart, who had been counting nuts and bolts. Mr. Gearhart whispered in apology to Melvin, "He's my best customer! He gets very angry if I don't wait on him at once!" So Mr. Gearhart hopped across the store to fish out the piano wire instead of waiting on Melvin.

"You look like a nice enough boy," said the Professor, in a friendly enough manner, wiggling his slippered foot impatiently while he waited for Mr. Gearhart.

Melvin was thrilled to be noticed by the great man. He also realized the Professor needed the wire in a great hurry.

Melvin cleared his throat. "Why don't I take your wire in my bicycle basket?" he boldly cried. "I can have it at your house before you get there yourself!"

The Professor smiled through his shaggy

beard. He came out of a faraway fog, for a brief instant.

"A marvelous idea!"

Forgetting about any bolts and nuts, without another word Melvin leaped onto the Silver Zephyr, the reel of piano wire in the basket, zooming off making a bee-line toward the Ketcham house. He parked the bicycle among the shrubbery, and bumped into the camouflaged green porch. From there he made his way cautiously to the green front door, and was waiting when the Professor came trotting up the street. (For an old man, he did not huff and puff very much.)

"Ah! So nice! You are HERE! Clumsy me! Forgetting to tell you where I lived!" exclaimed the Professor; and he started to reach for the piano wire.

"Shouldn't I carry it in?" begged Melvin anxiously.

"How thoughtful! I didn't think young

fellows were thoughtful any more!" said the Professor, unlocking the green front door.

Inside the old house it was very dim. The Professor lit a thick candle and showed him the way up and through the dark, dark house. At last they came to the ballroom, turned into a laboratory; the wide skylight lay over most of it. The sudden daylight pouring in was dazzling.

"Professor, put the candle out," suggested Melvin. The Professor, his mind probably on something else, opened a window and tossed the candle out.

"Give me! Give me!" said the anxious Professor—meaning the reel of piano wire.

Melvin handed over the reel, and the Professor took out a pair of tinsnips and started busily cutting off lengths of the wire, measuring it from his red-bulb nose to the end of his arm.

The Professor's laboratory was cluttered with gorgeous machines. Magnets. Leather pulleys. Rotating fans. Drill presses. Lathes. Generators. A dynamo. Melvin felt immediately at home, wishing he never had to leave.

At the end of the laboratory stood an electric player piano with lighted-up windows, featuring pictures of yellow ducks and white geese swimming on a pure blue pond. The piano was playing in ragtime.

Professor Mickimecki was fixing an attachment to the windmill on the roof. He forgot entirely about Melvin. So Melvin sat in an overstuffed armchair which was something like his father's own.

There was a polished wood knob at the end of each armrest. Melvin sat there idly clutching the knobs till the Professor was ready to notice him again.

Suddenly the armchair lurched—and started a bumpy trip around the room.

At once Melvin realized the armchair was controlled by means of the wood knobs. He fiddled with the knobs while the armchair

headed straight toward an experiment table
on which sat dozens of jars of bright-colored
liquids. You steered, it seemed, by adjusting

both knobs at the same time—still, Melvin was unable to slow the chair down. The chair narrowly brushed by the experiment table. The jars clinked and jingled noisily, the colored liquids danced a wild, wild dance.

The armchair kept going.

A great black leather pulley was spinning around, beyond the table, whirring and flapping.

The chair moved toward the pulley. Melvin turned the knobs, and the armchair, brushing aside stools and little benches from its path (Melvin had to keep swinging his legs up in the air), hurried next to greet a collection of batteries, celluloid strips, and metal discs laid out upon a stand. The armchair crashed against the stand, sending all objects flying.

But the busy Professor—about ten feet away—tying various lengths of piano wire, humming louder than the piano, did not notice what was happening.

The armchair lurched and slid (it moved

on rollers) and zoomed past Professor Mickimecki. Next, it skirted first one generator,
and then a second, bigger one. Melvin bit by
bit was getting skilled at adjusting the pair of
wood knobs—and, though things happened

quickly and new obstacles loomed before him, one after the other, he steered through the crowded laboratory on his dizzying journey with great success.

At last, Melvin got both knobs tight. Then, and only then, the armchair halted.

He sat there for a minute, blinking his eyes.

He was ready to start on another trip around. Slower, this time; he had a feeling he would figure soon how to control the armchair's speed. However, all at once, the Professor looked at Melvin sitting in the chair. He had finished fixing whatever it was with the piano wire.

"Such an excellent boy—not to touch anything. Just happy to sit there!"

Melvin blushed.

The Professor tugged at his beard. "Such a boy should be rewarded!" He rummaged around in a deep drawer in a cabinet marked LITTLE GADGETS.

"How would you like to borrow these?" he asked. "They are for reading, for looking,

when it grows dark. Really handy!'' The Professor brought forth a pair of thick-lensed goggles.

He pressed a tiny switch on the side; they buzzed, throwing out a steady, strong beam in front that Melvin could see even in broad daylight. Mickimecki's Electric Goggles.

Melvin accepted them with hands atremble.

"Or!" The Professor was rummaging about for a finer souvenir. "Would you rather go home by Automatic Shoes?" He brought out a pair of big yellow shoes, six wheels on each.

"No thank you," Melvin said. "I've a bicycle."

The Professor was reflecting; he seemed to be getting an inspiration. He was watching, also, with keen eyes the repaired thing turning through the skylight.

"Say—well—do you have a baseball?" the Professor curiously asked.

"Not on me. Back home. I think," Melvin admitted. He believed he remembered a baseball, still wrapped up, a birthday present, somewhere.

"So! Bring it with you, when you come

next. I will show something *interesting!* Good-bye!'' said the Professor, gazing at something near, that resembled a large soft-boiled-egg timer. His mind had drifted elsewhere again. He showed Melvin out, hastily locked the door, and disappeared inside the dark regions of the house.

Melvin walked out onto the lawn. Birds were singing. Had he really been inside? Yes: he found where the tossed-out candle had singed the green grass; a great brown-black patch had been made there.

A ragtime tune came tinkling out in the air.

Then—there was a shuddering of the vague, green-painted house. The dynamo was starting up. The dynamo, undoubtedly, got its source of power from a cold stream running far below the Ketcham house. The ground itself was humming and throbbing.

''. . . *When . . . you . . . come . . . next.* ''

Should I have told him I'm not just a

boy? Melvin was wondering. He fetched the Silver Zephyr out from under the shrubbery. He rode home pedaling swiftly, feeling small, next to the Professor, but feeling, too, as if he floated. . . .

There was his mother, trowel inhand, digging among the petunias, begonias, and zinnias in the flower beds. Emma Dudd was picking apples. Spunky watched the goldfish in the pond. His father was at the Ice Cream Works. Everything went on as though he had *not* met Professor Mickimecki.

Melvin's heart was beating like a violent drum.

That evening, just before it grew dark, Melvin stood at his turret window. He was wearing the Professor's Electric Goggles, switched on.

There was a quiet knocking at the door. It was Emma Dudd, who'd carried upstairs a piece of fresh apple pie she wanted an opinion on.

"Come in," moaned Melvin. His mind was far off, at the Professor's laboratory. Emma stepped in with mouselike steps, bearing a tray on which she had laid out a dish of thick pie, a fork, and a napkin.

She saw Melvin at the window sending out the goggles' rays.

"Scrambled eggs!" yelped Emma Dudd. *"His eyes has caught on fire!"* She went flying out of the bedroom, and the tray crashed in the hall.

Mr. and Mrs. Spitznagle hustled upstairs. Melvin took off the goggles. His parents ran into the room. Melvin *looked* the same as ever.

"I was just thinking—that's all. Is there any law against it?" Melvin asked. His parents went downstairs and cleaned apple pie off their shoes.

Their voices drifted up the stairs.

"We have a strange boy on our hands. We ought to face it," sighed Mr.

30

Spitznagle. "I face it every day," sighed Mrs. Spitznagle.

Melvin and Spunky went to sleep. The next morning Melvin hurried over to Professor Mickimecki's with the birthday baseball.

He parked the Zephyr again in the shrubbery. Then he located, carefully, the burned spot on the grass. Up above must be the laboratory.

"Pro-fes-sor!" Melvin called out. *"I've brought the baseball!"* And he threw it high in the air so that it would sail past the laboratory windows. Unfortunately Melvin's throw was too hard. The baseball plopped, with loud shattering of glass, onto the great skylight.

The crash brought the Professor's beard to the window. "Who is doing something?" the beard was demanding.

"It's me—the boy!" announced Melvin.

"Remember? I brought my baseball. Can I come up? Should I help sweep the glass?"

"Baseball? Baseball, BASEBALL?" The beard seemed to be confused.

"Baseball! Piano wire!" Melvin helped. "Yesterday!" The beard wiggled in a sort of understanding and disappeared from the window.

The green front door soon opened. The Professor emerged wearing a long smock with many stains upon it. "Ah! You brought your baseball! Excellent! How did you know I needed it?"

Next Melvin and the Professor were going up the stairs, two steps at a time. It was hard to do that in the dark.

"Where is this baseball you are bringing?" asked the Professor after they entered the laboratory.

"It's already *here*," Melvin told him. "I happened to send it through the skylight."

"So kind of you," said the Professor. The brand-new baseball lay on the floor.

The Professor nearly stepped on the baseball. He picked it up. He laid it on top of a worktable. He examined it—pinching it, rolling it with the tips of his fingers slowly across the tabletop.

As though tapping a small melon at the grocery, he tapped it until he found its soft spot.

"Do you mind?"

"Not at all," said Melvin.

With an auger the Professor bored a hole straight into the middle of the ball. Then he crammed some small gray metal pellets into the hole, using tweezers. With a crystal stick he probed, making certain no pellets were loose. He plugged up the end with quick-drying putty.

He rested the baseball on a round, copper ring.

Next, he sat on a stool in front of a small, black transformer which had two dials. He twiddled the dials, concentrating.

34

"Look!" shouted the Professor.

The baseball came alive.

Lazily it stirred upon the copper ring. Melvin was certain it moved—because the stitched seams of it slowly started to revolve.

The baseball floated up, off the copper ring completely. It made a slow, graceful

35

flight, up to the high ceiling, toward the broken skylight through which it had entered the laboratory. It danced around Melvin's head, leaped, spun, bounced, darting about like a wild insect. Then cautiously it approached the copper ring from which it began—circling, descending inch by inch till it rested, snugly, on the ring again.

The Professor shut off the black transformer.

Melvin walked over to the baseball and touched it. It was slightly warm. But not very much.

The Professor, pleased, smiled with yellow teeth through his beard.

Melvin wanted to ask many questions. Instead, he picked up the baseball (which was, after all, his) and began prying out the hard putty.

Thirteen little gray pellets spilled out onto his hand. He bit one and tasted it to see what it was made of. He spit it out and dropped it in his pocket; he would borrow it and give it back soon. Professor Mickimecki was sweeping up the broken glass from the skylight with a broom.

Melvin had pulled out pad and pencil and was scribbling notes at a great rate. He lifted up the black transformer, studying the fancy criss-crossed wiring underneath. He began drawing a diagram.

He was nodding his head, beginning to understand a bit, when the old gentleman looked up.

"Such an excellent boy—doesn't touch—"

The Professor dropped the broom with a clatter.

The old man tottered; the eyes above the shaggy beard shone in surprise.

"What have I *DONE?*" he moaned. "I have wandered halfway around the world, to get away from Peeping Toms! Children—even children—should not be trusted!"

He hurried to a cabinet, poked around, and took out a jar of dandelion wine. He poured it into a beaker and gulped it down. Through tear-dimmed eyes he saw Melvin still scribbling notes.

"So—look at everything!" the Professor groaned. "You might as well! All right, now you must go!"

The noon whistle whistled at the Tomato Cannery. It was afternoon. The sun was shifting. "We must talk sometime—man to man," the Professor added weakly.

Thin white clouds blew in the sky over the skylight. Black crows cawed a crow song. Melvin was edging toward the door. They could not speak man to man yet. Suddenly Melvin remembered: "I must bring back the Electric Goggles!"

"No, no. They are yours," the dazed Professor answered. "Let me keep your baseball. I would like to teach it how to fly—without starting from the copper ring. Unless—you know how to do that already?'' The Professor laughed anxiously.

"If I learn, I will tell you,'' Melvin promised him.

"Listen to me! It is difficult, this journey you want to make—to be a scientific mechanical wizard,'' the Professor warned, getting excited, giving Melvin a terribly wise look. "Better to have a farm. Grow chickens. Make omelettes. The simple life. Believe me!''

Melvin shook his head. "No—it's too late. I want to be a wizard. Like you.''

They said good-bye on the green camouflaged porch.

The Professor stepped down to the grass and watched Melvin pedal off. The Professor seemed to be standing on a very wide and spacious lawn, in his stained old smock, because you could not see the green-painted house behind him.

Melvin pedaled the Silver Zephyr

quicker and quicker; he let the warm after-noon blur, and the white breeze carry him.

The truck that delivered pies and cakes for Mrs. Goldsmith's Pantry Shelf blurred by. Clarence Root, the town plumber, followed, coming around, honking his horn as in a dream. Melvin was pondering the principle of the flying baseball. The time had come for him to think of doing something important. He wished he could dive right up into the air, flashing away from traffic.

Full of visions which began to be

sketched before him in the air, Melvin tunneled down the leafy streets faster—faster—and faster. He was imagining the colossal Professor Mickimecki standing out in an open field, surrounded by apparatuses and a great calliope, while he, Melvin Spitznagle, flew triumphantly over his head.

When he reached Bean Road, Spunky skittered out, miaowing, from under the verandah, to greet him. Melvin parked his bicycle and ran past the gray little cat into the

41

house, up into the spooky turret, to write some more notes down on paper.

Melvin did not step into his workshop until the plan and the theory were quite clear. Then, a light could be seen flickering from the barn at all hours. Melvin hardly slept, or ate, or spoke to his parents or to Emma Dudd. He walked through the house like a zombie.

One sultry August day a letter came to the Spitznagles from Aunt Lola and Uncle Gustavus and cousins Benny and Chester. They were planning a canoe expedition, with two seventeen-foot canoes, up the Manisaukee River some three hundred miles north— canoeing by day and camping out at night. They wanted Melvin to join them. They were to leave from White Feather City where they were renting the two canoes.

Melvin, who was really thinking of the project in the barn, poured sugar on his soft-boiled egg and listened with only one ear to his father's recital of the letter.

"Say! Isn't that something!" said Mr. Spitznagle, buttering the toast. "I envy you that trip! Golly! If this wasn't the peak ice cream season, your mother and I would be part of the expedition. Wouldn't we, Juanita?"

Mrs. Spitznagle showed her enthusiasm in a lady-like fashion.

"The main thing, it will be wonderful for Melvin. Won't it?" she asked, dipping into the cornflakes.

After breakfast, Mr. Spitznagle got out the map and traced the northern route of the Manisaukee.

"Wild forest country up there—there's a big rapids you shoot—pretty exciting, eh Melvin?"

Melvin did not agree.

He replied, "Sorry. I am otherwise occupied. *Nothing* could separate me from my

43

work. Not even tear gas," he added solemnly, and marched off to the barn, followed by Spunky.

"I wish Spunky could tell us what he's doing," said Mrs. Spitznagle.

"Juanita! The chance of his lifetime! A canoe trip up the Manisaukee! What will we write Gus and Lola? What is the matter with that boy?" growled his father. "Why doesn't he cooperate?"

Aut Lola and Uncle Gustavus, a few days later, telephoned Long Distance to coax Melvin personally. But he would not be budged out of the barn. He would not talk on the telephone. The answer to the telegraph to the barn was: UNABLE TO PADDLE CANOE. BIGGER THINGS AHEAD. HAS MY INTELLIGENCER SUPER-ACE TRANSFORMER ARRIVED YET?

And that was that. The canoe expedition left as scheduled, with no Melvin aboard.

Melvin asked his mother, soon after, for

a small black case of certain dimensions. "You might find something like that in the attic storeroom," Mrs. Spitznagle supposed. She went up with him to search. It was difficult to breathe, with all the stale, hot summer air which had collected under the high-peaked roof, but Melvin seemed not to notice. His mother sat near the small window, where robins had made a nest, fanning herself with an old palmetto fan. Industriously her son examined every ancient valise, overnight bag, case, and leather box.

At last he discovered, behind his grandmother's dressmaking dummy (which was wearing an old stovepipe hat owned by his great-uncle Edgar), a musty salesman's sample kit—a pigskin-covered box with a hinged lid and a latch. After he had shined it up and let it dry out, out in the open air, it was in excellent shape. Nobody knew whose it had originally been, or where it came from; how-

ever, for Melvin's purposes it was perfect. Almost.

The one disappointment was that the box was light tan-colored. Melvin had insisted on black. So he painted it with black shiny paint and picked off, with great care, the dead flies which got stuck upon its surface. When he was finished, he was very pleased.

On the hottest days Melvin remained in his workshop. He had rigged up some fans, and he wore his bathing suit at work, and in-between times he dashed through the lawn sprinkler under the boughs of the apple tree. He had also insulated the barn to keep it warm in winter and cool in summer. Therefore he was able to continue working at long hours on his project. A number of times he was tempted to ask the Professor's advice on details; but he consulted, instead, the many books in his scientific library.

"Melvin has more books than clothes," his mother would say unhappily. "Though I guess we should be thankful he is improving his mind."

For two days, Melvin repaired bicycles again. Word quickly got around—everybody

had developed some kind of trouble during the summer with their machines. Melvin set up shop on the elm-shaded driveway. A big sign announced CASH ONLY. Emma Dudd worked at his side, handing him instruments.

In this way he acquired cash to pay for the C.O.D. parcels that were arriving in numbers—small packages containing burners and beakers, scalpels and tweezers, magnifiers, chemicals, and whatnot.

He burst out of the barn, alarming his mother and some ladies who were sipping ice cream sodas on the lawn under Japanese umbrellas, one afternoon.

"I've discovered the secret of the gray pellets!" he roared with joy, dancing over the clover grass, doing handsprings. There were terrible lines under his eyes, however, from the long hours of concentration. The ladies murmured, sympathizing with his mother.

Apparently Melvin was going to apply the secret of the gray pellets—which made the baseball fly—to *something*.

It was Emma Dudd who noticed Melvin no longer rode the Silver Zephyr. If he had to go uptown to Gearhart's Hardware, it was by other means. Usually he wore his track shoes, though he did not mind riding uptown with his father. However, then he did not speak. He would stare out the automobile window mumbling to himself, or jotting down notes, or studying odd-looking diagrams he'd stuffed in his pockets. His father had a weird feeling while he was driving Melvin, as though Melvin were really an old man. One thing Melvin had to buy at Gearhart's was a can of bright red enamel paint.

Melvin took the black box up to bed with him, putting it under his bed at night. Sometimes the Spitznagles were certain they heard noises issuing from it as he passed in the hall—muffled clicks, whirs, and sputters. Spunky ran in the other direction at the sound of the black box. It was Tweet, Spunky's mother, who got used to it first. Spunky continued to regard the box with trembling whiskers, though later he began to get used to it.

"Where is the Silver Zephyr, son?" his father asked one evening, over his iced tea and dish of ice cream. "Don't you use it anymore?"

Melvin simply smiled—looking inscrutable—and carried his black box away.

Late one evening the Western Union messenger, Rudy Magill, came on *his* bicycle, bringing them a telegram from excited relatives. Aunt Lola and Uncle Gustavus and Cousin Benny and Cousin Chester had failed to arrive at their destination, at the end of the canoe expedition. They were three days overdue.

Melvin's mother fainted and Dr. Moots had to be sent for.

Melvin stayed up all the night, working feverishly out in the barn.

In the morning, he took a twenty-minute nap, then threw cold water on his face and went up to visit his mother, who was staying in bed (it was not her brother but Mr. Spitznagle's who was lost; all the same, the shock was affecting her greatly).

"Mama, please try to get out of bed,"

Melvin urged her. "I have finished the Box."

"What box?" his mother groggily asked from her mound of pillows.

"The Generating Stabilizing Electro Carbon Condensating Atmospheric Pro-Cyclonic Compact Dynamic Magnet Box."

"Oh?" she said. "What a clever boy."

"Come downstairs and I'll show you. I'm almost ready!" Melvin begged her.

So, with Melvin propping her up on one side, and Emma Dudd propping her on the other and carrying some pillows, they led Mrs. Spitznagle cautiously down the stairs and out to the back yard, where she sat upon a chair.

For the occasion, Melvin had changed to a clean suit of clothes and wore his Sunday cap.

Emma Dudd stood nervously by. An August breeze rustled the tree crowns. Melvin pushed open the huge barn door; he disappeared into his workshop. Some bugle music issued, at last, from within, played on a gramophone.

"The world's first Furious Flycycle!"
Melvin boasted, wheeling out his old Silver
Zephyr.

However, the bicycle was now painted
bright red; fastened above the handlebars was
the Intelligencer Super-Ace Transformer; a
fin or two had been added; extra batteries

were in cases on the sides; and, at the back, on the rear fender, was strapped the Generating Stabilizing Electro Carbon Condensating Atmospheric Pro-Cyclonic Compact Dynamic Magnet Box.

The Furious Flycycle.

Mrs. Spitznagle smiled weakly, from her pillow-laden chair. Emma Dudd exclaimed, in a loud whisper, "Scrambled eggs! I wish I had one of those for my afternoon off!"

"You don't think it will work, do you?" muttered Melvin.

He climbed aboard, switching on the transformer. There was an immediate loud racket from inside the black box on the rear fender. A crackling, a spluttering, a banshee-howling. Dwindling down to a series of small explosions.

Melvin started to pedal with demon fury. He smartly kicked the standard up.

Then—baroomp baroomp—he crashed—

slish, snap!—through the tall Norway spruces that lined the back yard. Having to push pedals and simultaneously to steer, and from time to time dialing the transformer, while listening to the many noises from inside the black box, kept him busy: he was not able to direct his gaze much, at first, up or down. He suspected his mother had fainted again; but he was too full of spruce-prickles to try anything more than to keep a straight course, in the air.

Emma Dudd screamed when she opened her eyes and saw that nothing remained behind of Melvin save his Sunday cap—atop one of the Norway spruces.

Mrs. Spitznagle was lying in a faint against the chair. Emma fanned her with her apron.

Melvin's ultimate destination was Professor Mickimecki's house.

He discovered that the most difficult thing was to keep his balance, since he was much heavier than air.

He slowed the Furious Flycycle down
when he got to that green-painted place.
Slower and slower he whizzed about the

house, bicycling over the laboratory's skylight, grazing the windmill.

The Professor glanced up, quite startled. The sound of a new machine had caught his ear. Melvin put on the brakes a bit, giving Professor Mickimecki a chance to rush out-of-doors.

He coasted over the Professor's head, sitting up straight (wishing he had his cap on to complete the picture).

"Now look at that. Oh look at that!!" the Professor gasped. "You have got yourself something there! I am congratulating you! Now tell me how you do it!"

The dazed old man wept. Pleasure and envy were written all over him. Melvin was unable to stop for a quiet discussion with the Professor; yet he had wanted the Professor to see the first ride.

"I must go home—I'll be back soon!" Melvin shouted down to him.

"Auf Wiedersehen!" shouted up the

Professor. "Speed with heed!" he earnestly
added, remembering a speck of advice he'd

picked up somewhere. "Ah, these young ones," sighed the Professor, rubbing his eyes with the end of his tie. "They must do everything right away, this minute! Johnny Jump-Ups! That's what they are!"

And he strained his ears listening to the moving Flycycle as it returned toward Bean Road—and shuffled, with worn carpet slippers flapping, back to an experiment which he had started in Stuttgart (or was it Prague?) thirty years ago.

Melvin nearly toppled over, twice, on his way back home. The Flycycle swayed precariously; Melvin leaned with his body just enough at once in the opposite direction. He became quite good at shifting his weight. He turned at the foot of Pumpkin Avenue, taking the long route home.

Several automobiles, on their way to work, chugged along underneath him, as their occupants tried to follow his path. Heads stuck out of windows. A few ladies on the sidewalks fainted.

Skinny Longnecker, Jr., who was crossing a vacant lot, shouted up some encouragement. Melvin made the mistake of waving to him, and lurched horribly; Skinny was openmouthed.

He practiced riding above the County

Fairgrounds, six times around the harness race track oval, until he was surer of himself. By shifting his weight backward, forward, to the right, to the left, and in combinations, he could cause the Flycycle to dip, bank, and soar.

By this time word was getting around town, and little groups of people were drifting toward Bean Road.

Melvin's father drove his car back from the Ice Cream Works. The crowd gathered in the Spitznagles' yard drew back when Melvin leaned forward, heavily, putting on the brakes, and landed handsomely beside his mother's begonias. There was a small ripple of applause from the crowd.

"*Now*—let me see that map of the Manisaukee River," Melvin instructed his father, eager to get going. His father had just found a spot to park in.

"He wants the map of the Manisaukee River," word was quickly passed along. Ev-

erybody had heard about the disappearance
of his Uncle Gustavus, his Aunt Lola, his
cousins Benny and Chester.

Mr. Spitznagle said, "Of course," then
dashed inside the house to fetch the map.

"Is he going to leave before lunch?"
Emma Dudd asked, wistfully. Melvin had

every intention of leaving at once—that was clearly written on *him*.

Emma scurried into the kitchen, to put up cold roast beef sandwiches and iceberg watermelon pickles. Mrs. Spitznagle came staggering out with Roman candles and rockets left over from the Fourth of July. "If you get lost, shoot these. Someone may find you," pleaded his mother. Emma ran out again with a bag of peaches.

"Thank you, Mama. Thank you, Emma!" said Melvin. He put the Roman candles and rockets, the sandwiches, pickles, and peaches, and the Electric Goggles inside his shirt. The crowd watched Melvin and his father poring over the map tracing the route of the Manisaukee. Spunky and Tweet stayed on the roof of the verandah.

Somebody volunteered to try shaking down Melvin's Sunday cap, atop the Norway spruce. Others felt it should remain where it was hanging, as a symbol.

Melvin bowed to the wishes of the crowd, letting the cap remain there, upon the branches of the spruce.

Melvin wiped off with a soft cloth the Furious Flycycle, until it gleamed; he checked the black box and the transformer, then got on.

It was a very hot day. He went up into, without any trouble, the brightest of summer skies. The spires of the town's churches reached toward him as he entered that other world, the world of the air. The crowd cheered! When he was able to look below, he was blocks away from Bean Road, within sight of the edge of town. The back yards of the small frame houses, where families grew neat rows of asparagus, beans, lettuce, and cucumbers, were different shades of green next to the green from the grass, the shrubs, the trees. In the yards, also, were riots of colors from planted flowers—asters, snapdragons, geraniums, hollyhocks, pansies, delphiniums, and

roses. Then he came to the County Fair-grounds, then the Old Folks' Home high on Shoop Hill, and at last the farm fields, where everything looked shiny, like smooth oilcloth.

The buzzes and whirrings from inside the black box were growing steadier; the Furious

Flycycle zoomed furiously along. He saw, whizzing by, the lush-growing crops laid out across the horizon—corn and wheat and soybeans and tomatoes, with tall clumps of trees rising between them. By shifting his weight he neatly leaped over these sudden barriers.

Gradually the land changed. The farms became less rich. He was riding over sparse potatoes-and-onions country. The soil looked dusty. Farmhouses lay further apart, the barns leaned at crazy angles, the buildings stood shabby and unpainted.

"Speed with heed!" the Professor had advised; that was pretty fair advice. So Melvin pumped and pumped—speeding with heed—following the route his father had marked on the map.

He came to high weeds. Wild grass. Scatterings of pine trees. Then, clumps of pines and cedars. He followed a stream which was part of the Manisaukee. He passed an ancient, ghostly, abandoned mill, all falling apart; its water wheel was broken. The boards that held the mill up had turned all silvery. He saw rabbits, foxes, and muskrats. He rode over thick forest country, where he heard the ring of axes. It was cool in the shadow of the trees. He rode the Flycycle low, so that he seemed to be just skimming the stream, because it was hard to follow its zigzag path from the air.

On a bank of wildflowers and brambles he settled down, eating his lunch of cold roast beef and iceberg pickles. Birds' cries echoed near. Bugs flew around his sandwiches and sat on his nose. Again he mounted his trusty Flycycle. The black box, which was overheated, sputtered and grumbled. Wrogga. Wrogga. Nnn, sssst. Nnn, sssst.

But Melvin did not think once about turning back: once you go ahead, you must go ahead.

He recognized—just where it should be—White Feather City. This was where his relatives had started, where the streams met

67

and formed the Manisaukee River. Here the Indians had long ago built an outpost. Beyond it was dark primitive country.

Melvin pumped the Flycycle. With more speed. With more heed. He felt he should ride as low as might be managed, almost touching the surface of the moving river, so that he would not miss a single clue.

At a point where the river grew narrow, making a channel, he came upon a beaver's dam. Here, his uncle, his aunt, and his two cousins would have had to ford the river and walk around. He glimpsed wide sloshy footprints in the mud at the edge. These might be Uncle Gus's, Aunt Lola's, Cousin Benny's and Cousin Chester's!

On he rode—and on—passing rapids so that he felt the spray of water splashing in his shoes. *Things* darted beyond the pines and the firs and other trees—the now-and-then maples, elms, and oaks.

The two canoes had passed through this very way that he was heading, swept along with the Manisaukee's current. Melvin thought about his missing relatives. He thought about them, hard. Aunt Lola played the piano and taught crocheting; Uncle Gustavus was in the soda pop bottle business; their sons Benny and Chester both had squinty eyes and were extremely uncoordinated; what chance would THEY have against the rolling rapids, against a sudden grouchy bear?

One thing—the whole family were champion swimmers: even Benny and Chester under water became like eels.

Melvin's legs ached from all that pumping.

Through the tops of the trees the sun flashed its gold. The day seemed to stretch on and on. Melvin pedaled vigorously. As he continued his search, he entered into the heart of a green wilderness (what did it remind him of? It reminded him of the green in which the Professor's house was painted), with only the sometimes wide, sometimes narrow ribbon of river running in-between. The water churned, spilling over huge, rough boulders flung down thousands of years ago by the Ice Age. At other times the water flowed peacefully, and the canoes must have had a smooth journey.

Vines and tangles tied the dark forest together. Trees sometimes crowded down to the water's edge, roots sticking out through the river bank.

The Furious Flycycle buzzed like a great red insect through that summer afternoon.

Suddenly he heard a horrible, horrible howling.

It was the howling of very bloodthirsty wolves.

Ahead of him he saw two beached canoes, like two great pods split open, with pieces of camping equipment—kerosene lanterns, frying skillets—spilling out.

A pack of wolves was gathered around a great oak tree. Up in the tree, sitting on the limbs, were Aunt Lola, Uncle Gustavus, Cousin Benny, and Cousin Chester. The tall wolves were dancing, some of them raised on hind feet, shredding off bark from the trunk with wild claws.

Aunt Lola and Uncle Gustavus and Cousin Benny and Cousin Chester all looked desperately hungry and very unhappy, out on the limbs.

Melvin slowed up the Flycycle, ringing his bicycle bell as he passed the big oak. The

Flycycle wobbled and chugged; he had to in-
crease its speed for fear of tipping. The
wolves snapped their teeth. They tore the

bark trying to get up, up into the tree. Melvin's relatives sat there with big, round eyes. They were unable to speak.

He gained altitude, going faster, passing over the treetops, then turned back, making a wide arc. He got out the Roman candles and rockets, lit them (that was difficult), and threw them down at the circle of savage wolves. "Hang on!" he shouted to his relatives.

The fireworks exploded with great popping sounds; the wolves yelped. Their fur coats got singed. Smoke poured forth. The beasts, frightened, plunged into the river. Melvin, by this time, made another loop around and he shot off the remaining rockets, aiming straight into the wolf pack. And they plummeted into the deeply tangled forest.

Melvin landed the Furious Flycycle under the oak. His relatives continued sitting high in the tree.

The wolves' red eyes, sharp teeth, loud howling disappeared into the far end of the

forest. "You can come down now. They are gone," he shouted up.

So, one by one, he helped them down.

They had been chewing on oak leaves; since they had not eaten for several days, they were as light as feathers. They all stretched out on a bank of moss, wiggling their stiff arms and legs. Melvin gathered nuts, gooseberries, and edible mushrooms. He brought out Emma's bag of peaches, which he'd saved.

His relatives lay there, eating the food. At last they were able to speak.

Aunt Lola studied Melvin with a quizzical eye. "Am I dreaming—or did I see you arrive on a bicycle?"

"That was me, all right. This is the Furious Flycycle. It is something I've been working on. It utilizes the principle of the Generating Stabilizing Electro Carbon Condensating Atmospheric Pro-Cyclonic Compact Dynamic Magnet Box."

"*That* is how you do it!" reflected his aunt. She turned to Benny and Chester, who were sprawling out two or three feet away. "Don't you wish you had half his brains?"

Benny and Chester sat up, blinking their four eyes. Both flopped down again. They were too weak even to think about it.

Uncle Gus came over to shake Melvin's hand, but he had to sit down, groaning a bit.

"We should be pushing off again," he said. "Melvin, we are mighty grateful for your help. My goodness—why don't you join our expedition? We would be happy to have you!"

Melvin realized they were in no condition to be pushing off. He suggested to his relatives that he take them back, on the Furious Flycycle, stopping first to visit his parents. His relatives scrambled to their feet, trying to reach the canoes. They couldn't make it. "Can we all fit on the machine?" wondered Benny and Chester hopefully; anything seemed better than rowing again, to them. The whole family, as a matter of fact, looked pretty exhausted.

"Yes, we can all fit," said Melvin. "I will think of a way."

Therefore he started to ponder. "With the added weight, however, we will require a pole to balance with—about sixteen or seventeen feet long.''

To whittle a pole out of one of the forest trees by means of a penknife would take nearly forever. With swift eyes he gazed about; he realized by tearing one of the canoes apart and using the center rib they would get a dandy pole.

So they helped him tear apart the canoe, and eventually they had a pole.

Still, he could plainly see *no* one was in shape to start the journey. It would take him a day, too, to teach them how to balance. Night was coming.

The full moon was shining. The frog orchestra was out in the river now. Soon they had a small campsite with a fire. The wolves had torn the tents to shreds. They lay on open ground with their heads toward the fire. Melvin handed them each a Roman candle, just in case. One of them, then the next, then the next, would stay awake an hour at a time, wearing or keeping handy the Electric Goggles.

In the morning they munched on gooseberries.

Melvin chose Uncle Gustavus to handle the pole. They found a clearing where Melvin was able to pedal the Flycycle round and round without leaving the ground, Uncle Gus sitting behind the seat, tied on with rope, since his arms had to be free for handling the pole. Uncle Gus did not get the knack easily. When he got it, his wife and sons cheered.

Then Aunt Lola had to learn to sit on Uncle Gus's shoulders.

Then Benny and Chester had to learn to sit; Chester on the crossbar, Benny on the handlebars. The best thing seemed to be to tie everybody on.

By this time it was early evening again. The sun fell lower in the sky, casting lengthy shadows. Melvin patted his Generating Sta-

bilizing Electro Carbon Condensating Atmospheric Pro-Cyclonic Compact Dynamic Magnet Box, encouraging it. The transformer buzzed. The black box coughed. Everybody was aboard.

The Furious Flycycle, a little the worse

for wear, was launched on its return journey. The sun got low and the sky got red, then violet, then darkish blue . . . and a bright comet zinged off in the distance.

The black box crackled, causing a frantic disturbance while Melvin pedaled the added weight through the air. Nobody spoke a word. Aunt Lola held onto Uncle Gus's ears. Melvin's legs pumped and pumped, without stopping, as if he were part of the machine itself. He took the straightest course home, steering this time by the Big Dipper. Summoning all his strength, he drove the Flycycle as fast as it would go. Mile after mile after mile.

A farmer and his wife were sitting out in the yard, on two rocking chairs. "Must be there's a storm a-brewing, Sue Ellen," the farmer reckoned, hearing the sound of whizzing (and Melvin panting) in the air.

"Nope. It's just folks afloating by on a bicycle, Harvey," she said.

They both decided to go into the house.

Melvin, Uncle Gustavus, Aunt Lola, Benny, and Chester rode on.

"Quit swinging your feet," Melvin had to tell his cousins sternly. "This is hard enough." "Sorry," they said.

Melvin's eyes were growing heavy. Everything was growing heavy. The Flycycle was proceeding less furiously. If only it would stay aloft!

"Here come some wild ducks," called Aunt Lola who was the lookout. It took all of Uncle Gus's paddling skill to manage the pole as they passed through the giant V-wedge of flying and startled ducks. The Flycycle went through a cloud of green and yellow loose feathers.

The Flycycle rapidly was losing power. In the nick of time Melvin spotted the lit-up Courthouse clock. The lady who stood in all kinds of weather on the copper roof, holding

up the scales of Justice, greeted them as they chugged by.

They coasted over Courthouse Square, aiming between the heads of the statues on pedestals, and Melvin pedaled down Bean Road, managing to keep a path in air, though gradually sinking.

People smiled and waved, and ran along with them. The High School band—which had been standing by—stepped out of the bushes and serenaded their return playing

Shine On Harvest Moon. His parents, who had been taking a walk and worrying, rushed forward. He shut off the transformer and lit upon the soft yard. Melvin and his relatives tumbled over, tied onto the Flycycle.

Untied, they posed for photographs.

Melvin leaned the Flycycle against a

gingko tree and patted it gratefully. "She got us through, thick and thin," he announced to the crowd and to the reporter from *The Evening Star*. Melvin and his relatives had to sit down on the front steps; their legs were pretty wobbly.

Emma Dudd thought of Baking Soda for their mosquito bumps. Aunt Lola told the story of how they had been held at bay by a pack of wolves until Melvin, on his machine, chased the wolves away with rockets, and how he managed to ride with four extra passengers. The crowd got hysterical at each mention of Melvin's name.

Then Emma shooed the curiosity-seekers off with a stiff broom. "Can't you tell they need REST? Why don't you leave them ALONE!" she scolded. So reluctantly the crowd backed away—though it kept waving and looking from the curb across the street. Mrs. Spitznagle and Emma scurried upstairs, preparing rooms for Uncle Gus,

Aunt Lola, Benny, and Chester. Mr. Spitznagle offered dishes, spoons, and a gallon of fresh tutti-frutti ice cream.

In the front yard there was a bearded figure, nodding its head in the moonlight. It had come over on a pair of Automatic Shoes. The figure whirred up the walk, holding its crumpled top hat in pawlike hand.

"How did you do it?" the figure asked. "That is what I must know."

"Please, everybody go in," said Melvin. "I must speak with Professor Mickimecki in private." They all went in and took their ice cream.

The Professor pulled his beard nervously.

The bushes sighed; a breeze stirred. The last of summer was in the air.

"I borrowed one of your gray pellets. I took it apart to see what it was made of. I made some of my own, then. Only better. Here is one. Do you want it?" Melvin fished

one out of a hidden compartment in his belt and handed it to the Professor. "The Furious Flycycle started from the gray pellet. Shouldn't wizards learn from each other?"

The Professor had to think about this.

He put the new gray pellet in his watch-fob pocket. He removed the Automatic Shoes (they were too tight to wear twice) and went off in stocking feet in the velvety darkness under the moon and the stars, toward his green-painted house.

The Professor's voice floated back in the dark.

"You planted the pellet like a seed! From that was growing something! Maybe we have something to talk about! Maybe we can work something out!"

The Furious Flycycle was rolled into the barn awaiting repairs. The workshop had never looked so beautiful.

Mr. Spitznagle came strolling outside again. He did not tell Melvin about the added big bills from Gearhart's Hardware. He decided Melvin was a satisfactory investment.

Mrs. Spitznagle stepped out. The relatives had been put in their rooms and were safely snoring. Since Melvin was tired, tired, tired—the pumping had worn out his legs— she fixed him a comfortable cot upon the verandah so that he would not have to climb the stairs.

Emma Dudd sat down in the kitchen. She was contentedly eating what was left from the tutti-frutti. What was left from that, she fed to Tweet and her son Spunky, quietly, in the moonglow.

Melvin's father and mother sat by his side till he had fallen asleep; and even then they continued to sit, out on the darkened verandah, holding each other's hand, listening to the cicadas chirping their night song.